ROBOT
SANTA

ROBOT SANTA

The Further Adventures of Santa's Twin

By DEAN KOONTZ

Illustrated by PHIL PARKS

HarperCollinsPublishers

Robot Santa: The Further Adventures of Santa's Twin
Text copyright © 2004 by Dean Koontz
Illustrations copyright © 2004 by Phil Parks
Manufactured in China by South China Printing Company Ltd.

For information address HarperCollins Children's Books,
a division of HarperCollins Publishers,
1350 Avenue of the Americas, New York, NY 10019.
www.harperchildrens.com

Library of Congress Cataloging-in-Publication Data
Koontz, Dean R. (Dean Ray).
  Robot Santa : the further adventures of Santa's twin / by Dean Koontz ;
illustrated by Phil Parks.— 1st ed.   p. cm.   Sequel to: Santa's twin.
  Summary: Bob Claus tries to make up for last year's Christmas havoc by building
      an android that can help his brother, Santa, by delivering toys in a gorilla-driven
        sleigh, but despite his good intentions, things go horribly wrong.
      ISBN 0-06-050943-0 — ISBN 0-06-050944-9 (lib. bdg.)
        [1. Robots—Fiction. 2. Gorilla—Fiction. 3. Santa Claus—Fiction.
          4. Christmas—Fiction.   5. Stories in rhyme.]
            I. Parks, Phil, ill. II. Title.
              PZ8.3.K842Ro 2004   [Fic]—dc22   2003022307

Typography by Carla Weise
  1 2 3 4 5 6 7 8 9 10 ❖ First Edition

Up, up at the top of the world, up high,
a dazzle of snow falls out of the sky.
The moment for takeoff is drawing nigh.
The well-trained reindeer are ready to fly.
Happy elves rehearse, now waving good-bye,
up, up at the top of the world, up high.

The great polished sleigh—see how brightly it gleams,
red as a cherry, as sleek as sweet dreams.
The bottomless bag of magical toys,
crammed full of wonders for good girls and boys,
onto the sleigh has been safely loaded.
It's been packed so full, it should have exploded.

By his hearth Santa drinks thick, hot mocha—
with sugar, some spice, a drizzle of cocoa,
cinnamon, nutmeg, plus two whiffs of cloves.
He eats pumpkin bread—four big orange loaves.
Not one sip or crumb must he be denied.
For his trip ahead, he must be fortified.

He pulls on his socks: two, three, four, five pair,
woven from golden—and real!—angel hair.
To certain angels, Christmas duty called:
They're happy to spend this holiday bald
to keep Santa's feet both toasty and dry.
(Don't worry, they'll grow new hair by and by.)

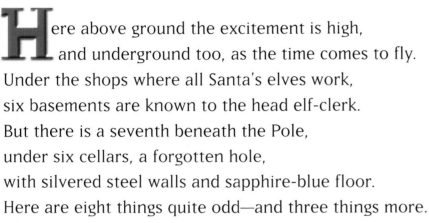

Here above ground the excitement is high,
and underground too, as the time comes to fly.
Under the shops where all Santa's elves work,
six basements are known to the head elf-clerk.
But there is a seventh beneath the Pole,
under six cellars, a forgotten hole,
with silvered steel walls and sapphire-blue floor.
Here are eight things quite odd—and three things more.

The eight oddities resemble reindeer,
usually creatures that no one need fear.
Yet these deer look weird, knobby, and blinky.
They sound so buzzy, beepy, and clinky.
They smell like fresh paint, like glue and fake fur.
They bark and gobble, moo, tweet-tweet, and purr.

Here too is a sleigh, as strange as the deer,
with a gorilla who has been taught to steer.
Magic makes Santa's sleigh zoom fast and high.
This sleigh lacks magic to make it fly.
It has radar and four rocket boosters.
Engine off, it still cackles like roosters.

Beside the sleigh waits Santa Claus—not quite.
This Santa is weird, he is not at all right.
He smells of oil and, stronger, of grease.
He wears cheap velvet and moth-eaten fleece.
Soon the real Santa will be much annoyed.
This is a machine! A robot! Android!

Santa's twin brother—Bob Claus is his name—
constructed this android. It's Bob we should blame.
He's clever with gears, cogs, wheels, and such stuff,
but as smart as he is, Bob's just not smart enough
to design, to build, and to program another
Santa as good as his most famous brother.

His motives are pure: He wants to assist
his busy brother, who has a long list
of stops he must make on this Christmas Eve.
Bob does not mean to confuse and deceive,
frustrate and annoy, or to be a pest,
but these are all things that poor Bob does best.

He also has trained the pilot gorilla
to work for ice cream—always vanilla,
and he named this robot Super Santa One.
Building the machine has been such great fun
that Bob never thought what might go wrong.
When will he find out? Well . . . not very long.

Bob plans to tell Santa, before Santa flies,
that Robot Santa will take to the skies
to deliver half of the toys and gifts
in spite of ice storms and giant snowdrifts.
First, the gorilla (his first name is Keith)
wants Bob to comb him, and floss his big teeth,
the better to impress the real Santa Claus.
He wants a bright smile when there is applause.

eanwhile, three thousand long miles to the south,
Charlotte lies sleeping with an open mouth,
snoring as no young girl should ever snore.
Her loud vibrations rattle the door,
rattle the windows, the floor, and the bed,
rattle the sugarplums a-dance in her head.

In the next bed lies a girl who is hissing
through a front tooth that lately went missing.
Her name is Emily, sister to Lottie.
Neither of these girls is ever naughty.
They dream of Christmas, of fun and fine gifts,
as past their window thick snow softly sifts.

L ast year their Christmas was ruined by Bob,
who stole Santa's sleigh and did a bad job:
delivering gifts like toad snot and cat poop,
a square basketball with a tiny round hoop,
a doll with six arms and wild crazy eyes,
a talking stuffed cat that told only lies.

They foiled Bob's plan to smear Santa's name,
putting an end to his dastardly game.
They returned Santa's sleigh to the North Pole
And freed the real Santa from the deep dark hole
where Bob had put him when Bob wasn't nice.
Poor Bob apologized not once but twice.

He had been jealous, envious, and rude,
not in much of a Christmasy mood.
When caught in the act, bad Bob did repent,
and all of his meanness just suddenly *went*!

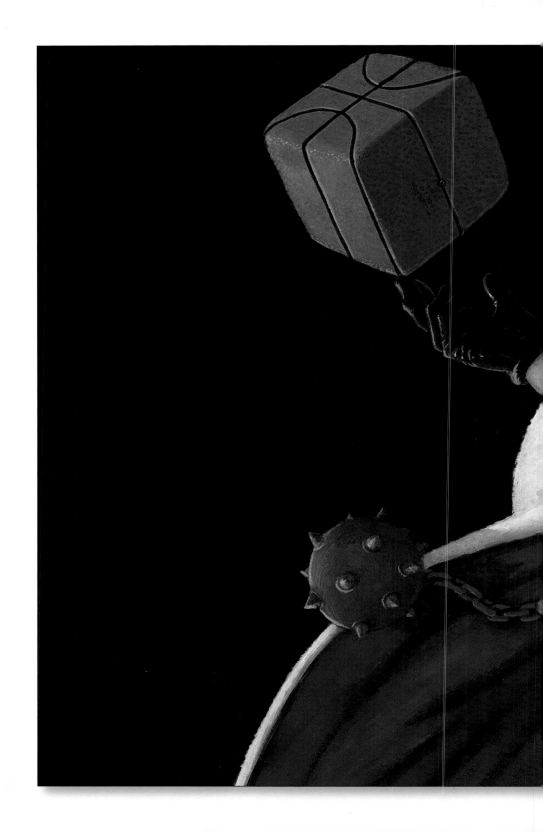

Curled up sweetly in a bed of his own
lies Woofer the dog, with a telephone
on which he tried to order tasty treats
like cookies, pickles, and various meats.
Though clever, he failed because it is hard
to purchase by phone with no credit card.

It's good that Woofer is alert and smart—
and, like all dogs, is a hero at heart.
Tonight he must be strong and courageous
to face events that will be outrageous.
Nice dogs will always do what is right
. . . unless they are foiled by their appetite.

Last year at yuletide, when Bob Claus was bad
—not just misguided—he made Santa mad
by giving the girls a gift-wrapped brown cow
as big as a car. Good heavens, just how
could such a huge beast be raised as a pet?
A cuddly puppy is better, you bet!

At Santa's request, Bob changed that big cow
into a black Labrador. He won't explain how.
He's not Santa Claus, only his brother,
but he knows some magic taught by their mother.

Woofer suspects Bob Claus will be back,
with new surprises in his big red sack.
He's heard the stories that the sisters weave
of the wild events just last Christmas Eve.

They say that bad Bob is better these days,
that he has reformed his mischievous ways.
But a good guard dog, though never malicious,
is without exception always suspicious.

From time to time to the window he goes,
and stands to look out on his tippy toes.
He studies the night in the whirl of snow,
listening to the wind huff, whistle, and blow.

As a bedtime treat, he received some sorbet,
lemon and lime—a fine end to the day.
If Woofer stops the nefarious Bob,
he'll get more sorbet, maybe corn on the cob.
At the night window he is heard to mutter,
"Maybe I'll get some smooth peanut butter."

Back at the North Pole, Santa says good-bye
to his wife, Bernice. She is ready to fly
to some fine five-star Hawaiian resort,
not pulled by reindeer that whinny and snort,
but in the private jet of Jack Frost, her brother.
Santa will join her with Tallulah, his mother,
shortly after dawn on this Christmas Day.
(The elves vacation in Pittsburgh, PA.)

Down in the seventh of seven subcellars,
the robot reindeer and other strange dwellers
watch the clockwork Santa clamber and clatter
into his jet sleigh. Something's the matter.
He shouts, "Merry Mishmash to one and all!
Happy Crumbcake! I feel shorter than tall!
On Dasher, on Dancer, on Prancer and Cupid!
I think my costume looks rather stupid!"

He's designed to be an efficient machine,
jolly, well-spoken, and not ever mean.
The first two names on his special gift list
are the young sisters—they must not be missed.
The plan is to give them presents galore,
which Bob Claus hopes will at last make up for
the chaos, confusion—and, yes, even fear—
that he brought them for Christmas the previous year.

Robot Santa's head rings loud like a gong.
Could it be Bob's plan has already gone wrong?

Robot Santa—or just "R.S." for short—
lets out a hiss, a squeak, and a snort.
The mad machine giggles, a sound that's not right.
The well-flossed gorilla responds with fright.
"Fruitcake!" cries the robot. "Marshmallow! Mutton!"
The spooked gorilla thumbs the wrong button.
"No!" shouts Bob Claus, but he calls out too late.
R.S. yells, "Cherry Mistmas!" sealing their fate.

BOOM-WACKA-BOOM-WACKA-BOOM-WACKA-BOOM!
The jet sleigh explodes straight out of the room.
The robot reindeer cough, hiccup, and sneeze.
The exhaust fumes smell like really bad cheese.
BOOM-WACKA-BOOM-WACKA-BOOM-WACKA-BOOM!
Through the launch tunnel, the jet sleigh goes *zoom*!

They rocket straight up through the snowy night,
scaring a polar bear so bad he turns white,
frightening feathers off some southbound geese,
trailing a dark cloud of oil and grease.
"Bingle Jells! Bingle Jells!" R.S. exclaims,
as through his head scroll addresses and names.
"Yappy Tuleyide! I know who's been naughty
and who's been good—like Emmy and Lottie."

Bernice and Santa peer into the sky
at the tumbling bear with the shock-white hair,
at the geese, at the grease, wondering why.
"This feels like Bob's work," Santa declares.

Down in the bottommost basement of all,
Bob's hat is smoking, his beard is too weird.
He's stumbled, tumbled, and taken a fall.
His boots are on backward, his pants are seared.

With hustle and bustle, eager to learn
what has just happened, and filled with concern,
Santa and Bernice arrive out of breath.
"Bob," Santa says, "you scared us half to death!"

Three thousand miles to the south of the Pole,
Woofer at the window smells trouble coming,
trouble much worse than a snake in a hole,
worse than a hive of angry wasps humming.

Charlotte and Emily sleep, dream, and snore,
while Woofer hopes he can help them avoid
the thing that all dogs most fear and abhor:
an out-of-control, freaky Santa android.

Keith (the gorilla, you may remember)
    sails on through the sky this night in December,
doing what no gorilla has done before:
driving a sleigh with gearshift on the floor.
The work is pleasant; the hours aren't bad.
This job is better than others he's had:
shoe salesman, lounge singer, cook, and plumber,
needlepoint teacher, florist, and drummer.

Drifting out of the stratosphere, they phase
into silent mode. They float down on rays
of golden light to the snow-covered roof.
Keith says, "Badda-bing!" (He is such a goof.)
The robot reindeer softly click, pop, and tick,
but they never get hungry, thirsty, or sick.
They never go toidy as real reindeer must,
though sometimes they do have problems with rust.

Super Santa One, the malfunctioning android,
steps from the sleigh and says, "You wait here, Floyd."
He means to say "Keith"—it's software trouble.
He folds himself once, then folds himself double,
slips down the chimney and into the house.
He frightens the boots off a Christmas mouse.
In the living room, by the holiday tree,
unfolded, he laughs, "Tee-hee, tee-hee-hee."

"Ho-ho, ha-ha-ha, ho-ho, hee-hee-hee,
noodles and poodles, blue moose and pink tea,"
says Robot Santa. "Just what is wrong with me?"

By the fireside, cake and cookies await
with Emily's note: SANTA CLAUS, YOU'RE GREAT!
This robot Kris Kringle eats only the plate.

From the mantel each girl has hung a stocking
brightened with sequins, beads, and flocking.
And Robot Santa just stands there gawking.

How big must their feet be! How huge their toes!
Such a girl must cause earthquakes wherever she goes!
Does each of these sisters have a ten-pound nose?

F earful of little girls with giant feet,
Robot Santa must make a hasty retreat.
He takes two quick steps but halts with a bleat.

A sprig of mistletoe hangs overhead.
If robots could blush, his cheeks would be red.
You cannot go now, says a voice in his head.

His brain is programmed with legend and lore
from two thousand Christmases and a few more.
When it comes to mistletoe, he knows the score.

Good manners require a sweet Christmas kiss,
a loving smooch in situations like this,
a tender moment of holiday bliss.

He unplugs his lips and kisses his cheek,
then nibbles his ear. Oh, dear, what a geek!
Forget *Robot Santa*. Call him *Santa Freak*!

Up on the roof in the sleek, red jet sleigh,
Keith quickly grows bored, with no games to play.
This job's not for him, and here's reason one:
He will not sit still when he could have fun.
For him "fun" means "food," a cake or a crepe.
So jolly, so hungry, this big hairy ape.

Out of the sleigh, across the roof he lopes,
seeking pancakes, pies. He has such high hopes.
He's looking as well for a friend to share
his adventures . . . and perhaps an éclair.
Gorillas, you see, are happy and hearty,
sociable fellows who like to party.

Hearing a low noise that sounds suspicious,
for once not dreaming of things delicious,
Woofer cranks open a casement window,
suspecting Bob Claus and needing to know.
To his surprise, a gorilla swings by,
grabbing his left ear—and away they fly!

Sitting up in bed, Charlotte says, "Oh, my!
Was I dreaming or did I really spy
a huge gorilla kidnapping my pup?"
From the other bed, young Emmy says, "Yup.
One big gorilla in a snazzy flight jacket.
Due to his size, I expected more racket."

The sisters are not mystified or afraid.
They know what's next in this silly parade.
Bob Claus is reformed—this much may be true—
but that doesn't mean he will always do
the wisest, safest, most sensible thing.
Lottie says, "It's Bob." Em says, "Badda-bing!"

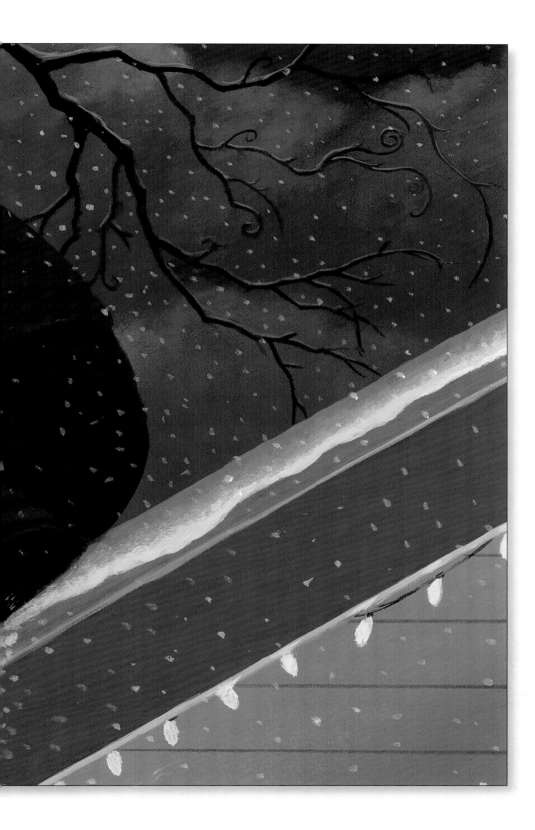

From roof eaves to tall trees, the gorilla swings.
   This is not one of Woofer's favorite things.
He prefers four paws flat down on the ground.
He is, after all, not a bird but a hound.
Tucked under the ape's big burly left arm,
He flies through the snowy night with alarm.

The dog is prepared to stand and defend
Emmy and Lottie—to the bitter end.
The key word is "stand," but he's in midair.
It's not easy to fight while flying up there.
His predicament puts him in the mood
(as usually he is) to dream about food.

Though fearful of bumps and bruises and cuts,
Woofer asks, "Do you have bananas, peanuts?
What else do gorillas eat in the wild?
Myself, I like things both spicy and mild:
sausages, eggs, toast with butter and jam,
marshmallows, muffins, a thick slice of ham."

The gorilla burps—sounds like a big frog—
and says nothing more. He doesn't speak dog.
Behind the house, he descends to the yard.
Dropped by the ape, Woofer doesn't land hard.
He drifts quietly down through falling snow,
'cause he's a smart dog who's learned to fall slow.

Sneaking down the stairs, alert and wary,
Lottie and Emmy cautiously carry
defensive weapons, but nothing that's worse
than a pom-pom slipper and a pink purse.
In the living room, they find that old scamp,
Bob Claus, holding a ginger-jar lamp.

"What's your gorilla done with our sweet mutt?"
Emmy demands and kicks Bob in the butt.
But when the Claus turns, he's not who they thought.
He's a ticking, clicking, wild-eyed robot.
He's herky and jerky and clearly man-made,
and appears to be eating their fine lampshade.

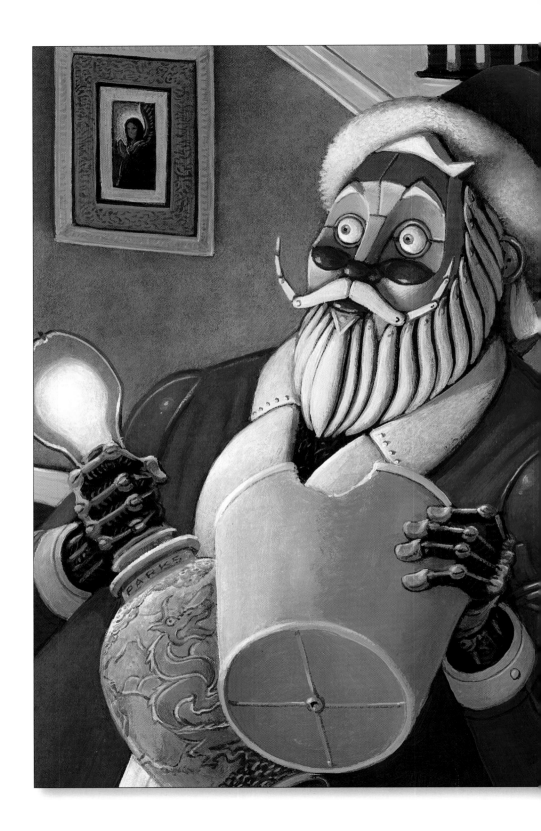

"You left lots of cookies but only one plate,"
mumbles the robot, "and I want more to ate."
"You mean 'more to *eat,*'" Lottie's quick to correct.
Bob Claus built this weirdo, the girls both suspect.

Looming scarily, it growls, "Ate or eat,
ate or eat! Hey, you girls *don't* have big feet."
They don't have big feet, but they're smart and tough.
They won't take any of this robot's guff.

Em says, "Put up your hands, spit out that lampshade.
A citizen's arrest has herewith been made."
Lottie says, "You're off to jail—or to the junkyard.
I'll tie you with tinsel. Emmy, stand guard."

"Out of my way!" cries the robot, with drama.
"Or I will tell icky lies to your mama.
I'll tell her you eat worms and crawly bugs.
I'll tell her you're two small-footed young thugs."

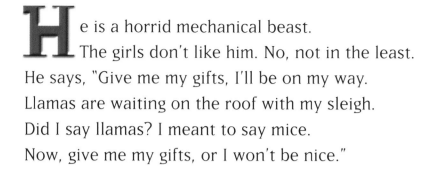

He is a horrid mechanical beast.
The girls don't like him. No, not in the least.
He says, "Give me my gifts, I'll be on my way.
Llamas are waiting on the roof with my sleigh.
Did I say llamas? I meant to say mice.
Now, give me my gifts, or I won't be nice."

He's got it backward. He must give, not take.
This is not Bob's plan. This is a mistake.
Perhaps it's caused by frequency jamming,
or one small error in the programming,
far too much grease or not enough oil,
sand in the gears or rust on a coil.

"Box up the TV and that nice knickknack,
the mantel clock, yes, and some bric-a-brac,
that ginger-jar lamp . . . hey, who ate the shade?
Give me all the money that you've ever made.
Give me your slippers, and those two fine chairs.
Next I'll go see what I want from upstairs."

Suddenly sparks shoot straight out of his nose!
Hot crackling currents curl both his boot toes.
Colorful auras flare over his head.
"If I weren't so busy, I might lie down in bed.
But this is Christmas, and I've much to do—
I'll take that sofa, that tea table too."

Keith, the gorilla, enters the kitchen,
a place that he finds simply bewitchin'.
Cinnamon cookies perfume the sweet air.
He smells cake too, and a fresh-baked éclair!
Having been a florist but also a cook,
he could bake any treat without a cookbook.

Woofer watches from the open back door,
ready to wrestle the ape to the floor.
But Keith (also a plumber) in a wink,
fixes a bad drip in the kitchen sink.
He ties on an apron, dons a chef's hat,
then gets out the sugar and the butterfat.

This dog is tough, and he has a brave heart,
but he's also hungry and pretty darn smart.
He knows the difference between a villain
and a gorilla who's able and willin'
to whip up something that's tasty and sweet
for a newfound friend with four furry feet.

Emmy and Lottie refuse to let go
of the tea table or sofa, and so
the robot whistles for reindeer assistance.
A rattle of hooves comes from a distance.
Without a knock or a ring of the bell,
reindeer burst in, and they sure don't mean well.

Their laser eyes glow, hooves *click-click* like steel.
They appear to be hungry, in need of a meal . . .
maybe Emily Salad, Lottie Stew.
There's no telling what robot reindeer might do.
Out-of-control robots are not often nice.
Fortunately these are afraid of mice.

That Christmas mouse, once scared out of his boots,
reappears here with squeaks, hisses, and hoots.
Growling and snarling, he makes quite a show.
He can't hurt steel reindeer, but what do they know?
This tiny terror sets the deer on the run.
Such clatter! Such chaos! But also such fun!

The gorilla chef, in a tall white hat,
finds ice cream in the freezer. Imagine that!
One quart of strawberry, one of mint chip.
Two of vanilla! See his chef hat flip!
Vanilla, vanilla, vanilla, oh!
The gorilla is happy—totally so.

In the wink of a finger, the snap of an eye,
Keith gives Woofer one quart and they apply
bright busy spoons to big bowls of this treat,
drenched in butterscotch syrup so thick and sweet.
The problems between them mean nothing now,
as they enjoy this wonderful gift (from a cow!).

(Yes, a dog has no thumbs and can't use a spoon,
but then—hey, diddle-diddle—cats can't fiddle
and no cow has ever jumped over the moon.)

hen a reindeer slams through the swinging door,
one robot reindeer, two, three reindeer—more!
Pursuing the deer is one angry mouse.
Now Robot Santa, that malfunctioning louse,
follows the rodent and is followed by
Emmy and Lottie. They all seem to fly.

The kitchen is noisy, much like a zoo.
They can't all fit in here, but fit they all do.
'Round the table, the mob whirls with a roar,
some on the ceiling and some on the floor.
All of a sudden they're gone like a dream—
but so are the bowls of vanilla ice cream.

Keith howls with dismay and at once gives chase,
as Woofer does too, all over the place:
living room, dining room, parlor, and hall.
Dash away, dash away, dash away all!
Fast up the staircase, but fast down again.
Then upstairs once more. It makes your head spin!

Over Emmy's bed, then under Lottie's.
Now through two bathrooms, around sinks and potties.
Into the bedroom where Mom and Dad sleep
the chase continues but without a peep.
Here they run silent, and leap in a hush,
shouting in whispers to each other, "SHUSH!"

Mother and Father sleep on unaware,
as robot deer ricochet here and there,
as Woofer bounces and as Keith careens,
as the girls tumble—a really weird scene.

Through a window and right out the room,
the chased and chasers go za-za-zoom,
onto the porch roof, up a ladder of snow,
to the top of the house, with not one ho-ho-ho.

From chimney to chimney (this house has two),
they squabble and flail, all without a clue
that they look absurd, silly, and even mean,
less like Christmas and more like Halloween.

A silver spotlight strikes down from on high.
Everyone freezes, looks up at the sky.
A voice from above says, "Desist and cease!"
Hovering above are the North Pole Police.

North Pole Police are big fluffy white bears.
No one sasses them; oh, nobody dares.
They don't carry guns, only big candy canes.
Not just all muscle, they've also got brains.
They don't use force on any occasion
because they have great powers of persuasion.

Hovering in their blue-and-gold police sleigh,
(which doesn't require reindeer, by the way,
because it's an antigravity machine)
the bears look stern, but they don't look mean.
The candy canes fire soothing sweetness rays
that make a grouch or a robot all smiley for days.

Only Robot Santa is badly affected.
If he has a smile, it can't be detected.
He spits out a bolt, sneezes two bent springs,
coughs up a piston and other strange things.
To Emmy he says, "I want that tea table.
I'm gonna chase you as soon as I'm able."

Lottie says, "No way," and the bears activate
electromagnets that at once levitate
Robot Santa and all his robot reindeer,
attaching them by hoof, nose, hand, and ear
to the rear of the North Pole Police sleigh.
Then without sirens, they're up, off, and away.

Behind the bear cops, the real Santa arrives,
in a magnificent sleigh, which he drives
with one hand while he waves with the other.
Beside him sits his troublesome brother,
looking embarrassed, rumpled, slightly charred.
At the sight of Bob, the girls are on guard.

Without harm to dog, gorilla, or girls
Santa lands on the roof, and the snow swirls.
"Emmy, Lottie, you look one year older!"
Santa says, and claps each on the shoulder.
"My brother is older too, but for sure
he is not even one day more mature."

Bob blushes, shuffles, and says, "Sorry, kids.
I had a good plan, but it just hit the skids.
I'm changing my ways. This is a new start.
I'll not just be good—I'll try to be smart.
No more androids, no more reindeer machines.
That isn't the stuff of good Christmas dreams."

"Christmas," says Santa, "is about living
your life with love and a spirit of giving,
friendship, compassion, peace, and bright hope.
All that's more important than how to cope
with a long gift-list and too little time.
A robot Santa—he's not worth a dime.
The spirit of Christmas requires, very much,
gifts of the heart and a personal touch."

"Keith," Santa says, "you're herewith deputized, honorary elf. Now let's take to the skies!
We've places to go and giving to do.
I don't think I'll make it without help from you."
Keith grins with delight. This is his great dream.
He won't even ask to be paid in ice cream.

Santa has a task for the sisters too:
"I'm giving custody of Bob to you.
I want him to do community service.
He's on parole. Now, don't be nervous.
He must do exactly whatever you say,
and not be troublesome in any way.

"For one month my brother will make your beds,
polish your shoes, brush the hair on your heads,
keep your room clean, and do all of your chores.
He'll make tasty cakes, pies, cookies, and s'mores.
He'll give Woofer belly-rubs day and night
and won't do anything that isn't just right."

With a "ho-ho-ho," and Keith at his side,
Santa sets off on his celestial ride,
up into the night, up into the snow,
leaving the girls on the roof far below.
This Christmas Eve is tick-ticking away.
Soon will arrive a bright new Christmas Day.

Although Bob sheds a tear of contrition,
Woofer regards him with deep suspicion.
The roof is so high. The sisters both frown.
Emmy says, "Bob, you must carry us down."
"Of course," Bob replies. "Whatever you say.
I'm here to assist you in every way.

"But wouldn't it be grand," he adds with a sigh,
"if we could build a time machine and fly,
back into the past, until just yesterday,
and stop the robot before it went astray?
If I could turn time back, back on itself,
I could please my brother, that jolly old elf.

"Of course," Bob continues, "I'll need some cash
to purchase equipment and establish a crash
research program to manipulate time.
I'll need major bucks." Em says, "Not a dime!"
Lottie says, "Not from me, the dog, or the mouse!
Now it's time to go down and clean the house."

The stockings are hung by the chimney with care.
Bob has a schedule: brush Emily's hair,
rub Woofer's tummy, then take out the trash,
whip up some s'mores (add sprinkles for flash),
vacuum the carpet, then slice some good cheese
(for the brave Christmas mouse, if you please),
rub Woofer's tummy, scratch behind his ears,
shovel snow off the sidewalk, brew some root beers,
rub Woofer's tummy, polish Charlotte's shoes,
entertain the girls by singing the blues,
by juggling cook pots, by dancing ballet,
by writing a humorous musical play.
All this Bob must do while being discreet,
because he must not accidentally meet
Emmy and Lottie's father and mother,
who won't understand that Santa's brother
is just as real as Santa Claus himself,
and who might be panicked by this big, bearded elf.
So while he does chores, he slips, slides, and sneaks,
ducks behind furniture when the floor creaks.
He never slurps when he samples root beer,
and he whispers softly, "Merry Christmas, good cheer!"